This text is partly non-fiction and

At the end of the text (in the notes/c. , - explain what parts of the short story are my views and what parts are just for entertainment.

1. Final Days

By the time of the start of 2024 the Tory Party had become a complete irrelevance. They were a rabble. They were a bunch of individual narcissists. Clearly they didn't care about the people so it is to be expected that they were not doing a good job for the masses. But this rabble were not even doing a very good job of serving the Propaganda State. That meant they were not doing a good job of serving their own institutional power. Even in their own view they were at best going to become a small party scoring around 20–25% support and at worst they were going to become a tiny party (practically extinct) and competing with the Greens and Lib Dems for support.

Robert Sutton, Sarah Pickering and Barry Willis are chatting in the Turners Mill Pub in Redcar. Robert is a Sociology tutor, Sarah makes money in various ways online and Barry is a short story writer.

Barry Willis says "The Labour Party needs to change its name to reflect what it really stands for. 'The Tory Wets Party' or 'The Centre Right' or 'The Liberal Right' are my helpful suggestions. Meanwhile a Democratic Socialist Party should be created."

Barry said that within a societal context whereby people were increasingly radicalized and wanted the entire lot of Westminster to simply f-off. That might sound blunt but it is a fair reflection of how people were thinking.

Barry continued…

"A continuity Tory Party will get treated like a continuity Tory Party. Its not the colour of a rosette that people judge. Its the policies!"

The irrelevant blue Tories were meanwhile splitting in two. For a long time they had been two factions: A Liberal Tory faction and a Reform UK faction. Now they looked to be heading to a future of two different parties. But all of this was shit for the toilet. The gigantic turd that had been blocking the toilet for over 150 years was about to be flushed!

"Have you noticed that the right wing are always on the wrong side of history? On free education, free healthcare, universal suffrage, higher education for the working class and for women and so on?" said Robert.

"I know why that is" says Sally. "It's because they exist to defend privilege. That is why they are called Conservative. It is a defensive position. And it is why progressives can always claim to have been on the right side of history. Because whenever those status quo defensive positions are breached, then progress is made and the progressives feel validated."

"So you are anti Tory and pro Labour…"

Sally interrupts.

"I am anti Tory but not pro Labour. Because the latter have never even bothered to try and be anti power for themselves. They have tried (at times) to come across as redistributive in terms of income and wealth… albeit never anywhere near to the Scandinavians… but in terms of power they have not. They are almost as shite as the U.S. Democrats. Basically Labour and the Democrats talk left, act status quo. Its not 100% like that, but its not far off. At least the Tories admit they hate us."

So you are anti Tory and anti Labour?" asks Robert as Barry goes to the bar to buy a drink.

"I am anti Tory. I refute that there is any such thing as Labour, except in name."

Here Sally is getting close to arguing that we live in a Propaganda Matrix.

"You know what the worst thing about the right wing is?" says Robert.

"Hell no! There's too many contenders to know where to start!"

"Its when they whine about positive discrimination. And the reason that is so bad is because it is an avalanche of hypocrisy. They whine about a tiny bit of positive discrimination while simultaneously defending a system that allows people to be born into vast privilege… the ultimate positive discrimination. Much of the working class' goal is to end that privilege, that mountain of positive discrimination and to allow the potential that is in the working class to flourish. But we cannot do that if we just block any change just because the privileged are obsessed with not doing anything for opportunity. So if we had listened to, rather than fought against the right wing, we would still have a world where women and working class couldn't even read and write. But because we didn't just accept that is their place, it is now common sense that they are detectives, scientists, academics. and so forth."

"It is ironic that the left are to be credited with Margaret Thatcher becoming PM." Robert eye rolls at Sally's point but agrees with the general point being made.

"Yeah, but in 99.99% of cases overcoming the status quo has been a good thing" replies Robert.

"And in the present day the right wing are still blocking the distribution of wealth. power and income."

Barry returns with his beer but he is distracted by the Middlesbrough v Chelsea Carabo Cup match being shown live.

Robert outlines the basics of what and why he thinks as he does.

"People in everyday society tend to act as equals to one another… when they meet in the streets, cafes, pubs and so forth. Its power politics where splits happen. And that is where they create power inequality. Some of it poisons and brainwashes a few peoples minds. But even that seems to be cured when people come together. So in the University settings you find equality culture. In focus groups you find equality culture. In Juries you find equality culture. And something very serious such as medial science is for all. No wonder medical scientists are overwhelmingly left wing. Equality is the solution. Equality means no split off cliques. Einstein supported equality and socialism. And philosophers, artists, writers from down the ages have been, far more often than not, pro peace and equality. Very rarely are they associated with right wing beliefs! And yet had the right wing been more successful throughout history the working class, including myself and yourself, would still be illiterate!!!"

Sally shouts "HERE HERE!!! I am really enjoying this. Continue on Rob!"

"Ok I will. Still with the basics. I'm anti politics as we know it. I think we should get society sorted out so that it is not poisoned. We need it to be By the People for the People. At present it is By the Power Corrupted split off Clique for the Power Corrupted split of clique. Some people have started to refer to the Propaganda State. It sure is that! Continuing with the basics… there's just people.

I'm not anti Tory people. And obviously I'm not anti
Labour people. But both can support the Propaganda
Matrix, vast inequality, war, deprivation, and policies
leading to premature deaths and untold suffering of both
the psychological and physical kinds. Both can be blamed
for suicides and crippling illnesses of multiple kinds,
leading to a time in history that will be remembered as
mentally unsound. This is because their minds have
brainwashed and even seeing through that brainwashing
doesn't mean that they now know the way out. They are
still not completely free."

Sally interrupts… "We've all been there!"

"True you interrupter." Rob continues… The reason I'm
not anti Tory people and not anti Labour people (except
for those at the top in both cases who play the power
game) is because of what I said before. When people come
together they act equally. That destroys all of that babyish
gaslighting. Its socially sensible whereas gaslighting its
immature and for f-ing kids, politicians and some national

reporters who haven't grown up. It is the power politics at Westminster that is the poison. Also you don't so much need to put people in focus groups or study groups to realise this. Its largely true and observable in everyday society. As said in the streets, in the cafes, in the pubs. But when people come together in study groups, focus groups, Uni settings, Juries… then its overwhelmingly true. Onto the next point concerning these basics… the working class has the best sense of what is required to happen because they are the one's who suffer the most. Thus there's a class solidarity in me but it isn't anti middle class because as said, when people come together there is a solidarity there. Moreover we would all like to be a middle class professional. Its just about not kicking the ladder down when you get there. When I was younger there was more kicking the ladder down after people had climbed it than there is today. So it is Westminster that is the violent institution that does divide and rule, that prevents all that I support and threatens me with my worst nightmares such as more divide and rule, thus more propaganda and even with nuclear holocaust. They pour more and more poison into society because they are addicted to doing so."

Sally interrupts again saying "Hey, I think we would agree with a basic description of the Propaganda State… or Propaganda Matrix as some call it. The Propaganda State is the Westminster political class, government, political parties and the national news media. All of that is a self-serving cartel, supporting themselves and supporting multi millionaires and billionaires while using the public for their own power and control."

Robert stands up and claps and simultaneously says "Sally, that is so good that I am buying you a drink!"

As Robert walks away Sally shouts "Have you noticed that they get bored of getting at someone like Putin, some even start to really like him so they switch their enemy?"

"Yeah" shouts Robert back and adds "Never jump on that evil bandwagon. Warmongering is used to deflect. Remember that no war other than class war."

It is half time in the Cup match. Middlesbrough are winning 1–0 in the semi final first leg. The TV channel has now being switched over to Sky News and Sally shouts over to Robert

"Look at the TV screen news… looks like the start of a civil war."

Scuffles with the Police has broken out over multiple UK cities with people wanting the collapse of not only the Tory Government but also the State Superstructure per se.

With it being half time Barry Willis rejoins the conversation.

"Too often the centre left have merely argued for policies such as and extra twenty quid on Universal Credit or a bit more on family credit/child credit. Its not good enough to say its a compromise. It's insulting. Compromise sounds like a nice word but fairness shouldn't compromise with a system that is so unfair and corrupt. If you leave the Propaganda Matrix in place then you are complicit in current and future evil. For example you might get future far right extremism. You might get future nuclear war. You most certainly will get continued manipulation of the working class. The reason for this is because the Propaganda State exists for itself. It is a split off clique. If you focus on the party political game, i.e., a game played by the split off clique, then that is to fall into their trap. Electing Keir Starmer falls into their trap. He will just defend the status quo. He is pro Propaganda State."

"What are we asking for though?" asks Sally.

"We are demanding more from ourselves. We should be like Gramsci!" says Barry guessing the right answer.

Robert isn't impressed.

"Cut the name dropping. These cliques that go in for that Marxist stuff lose the people before they even start to win them over. People are with us as we are."

"Go on... expand" says Barry.

"Right. People are with us on the distribution of power, wealth and income. The Propaganda Matrix has to throw out a ton of propaganda to get anywhere near to changing that. But they can't anymore because they have been seen through. But for gods sake, those groups that give themselves pedantic names... if they get anywhere near to a megaphone, then they are alien to people and they are therefore more like an enemy than on our side. I think Gramsci talk encourages them."

"You mean like Marxist?" asks Barry.

"100% yes."

"I agree. And besides, its not about Marxist policies anyway" says Sally before walking to the bar to buy herself and Robert a drink.

"Correct. Its about the People deciding. It is just obvious that, given that the people are not a self-serving clique that would do divide and rule against themselves, that they would be a hell of a lot more egalitarian" explains Robert before clarifying…

"Or we need a Constitution that ensures a fair society. We can have discussion and debate within that context. But a power tripping, manipulating Propaganda State should be illegal."

"Yes. And another point… I would support a counter revolution against a Soviet style communist takeover. I mean the 20th century Soviet Union was a hugely centralized Propaganda Matrix. Exactly what we oppose."

"A split off power clique, armed with nukes, pointed at the U.S. which would have led to our deaths in the UK too."

"All we demand is equality. And yet we get shit pies slammed into our faces 24/7, 365 days a year for it."

"Well its time for the largest shit pie ever to be splatted at 1 million miles an hour into all the Rupert Murdoch's of this world, and the very similar Daily Mail owners, and the Propaganda Matrix per se."

"Absolutely with cherries on top!"

"You mean cherries on top of the Shit Pie?"

"Ha!"

Robert goes to the toilet and the conversation continues with Barry and Sally.

"The reformist left uphold the propaganda Matrix when they buy people off with scraps." says Sally.

She's always found the reformist left to be fake and more interested in the Propaganda State's power and control than anything else.

"Exactly, and given that the right do that as well, then it demonstrates that its a cartel. As we were saying, Starmer is Pro State. Blair was and is Pro State. Wilson was Pro State."

"What about Atlee?" asks Sally wondering how Barry would deal with a challenging question.

"1945 was an exception to the rule. Given that millions of people had their legs and balls blown off, and were suffering from bereavement and massive Post Traumatic Stress Disorder, even the Propaganda Matrix had enough of a social conscience in that context."

Barry passed the test to the challenging question in Sally's view. But she does think that Barry may have overlooked that not all of the State were onside in 1945.

"Yeah, it shouldn't take a world war to grow a social conscience. But not all of the Propaganda State grew a social conscience back then. Check out the right wing press during the 1945 election campaign. They were calling Labour a bunch of commie, trot, Marxist, Soviets. If you check those newspaper headlines now it reads like it was… i.e., propaganda on steroids."

"It failed. The Propagandists had temporarily been well and truly seen through."

"Yeah, and given the right wing converted a few years later by their own logic they became Marxists themselves."

"Ha Ha! True. That exposes them as propagandists! But note, while the people had seen through the Propaganda Matrix in 1945 it was because they had seen just what the State is capable of during World War 2. So the bullshit that those right wing rags you mentioned was easy to see through. But the Propaganda Matrix just had to bide its time. The 1945 moment was just a moment. If you don't deal with excessive power then it is just going to assert its ugly face again further down the line."

"Yup. And we aren't claiming to be saints. No one's heart has to bleed. Its just about fairness that's all. No one has to be a saint. We don't have sleepless nights do we? But we still know the difference between justice and injustice. We still know the difference between privilege and fairness."

"Well we are a trillion miles away from that. We have billionaires. But then as Sir Michael Marmot, said We're starting to suffer Victorian diseases.. Universal Credit pays 70% of the cost of essentials.. If you're on Universal Credit [and no other family members are supporting you] we guarantee you will get sick because we don't give you enough money to [both]eat healthily, [and] to heat your home" "Britain has become a poor country with a few rich people.. It's worse to be poor in Britain than in most other European countries. Poor people in Britain have a lower income than Slovenia'"

Robert returns. He says…

"And Labour's answer… continue Tory policies."

"Labour should just be called the Tory Party" states Sally.

"And what should the Tory Party be called?"

"The Tory Party."

"But then we wouldn't be able to distinguish between the two."

"Exactly."

The second half of the football starts and Barry focuses entirely on the match. Sally says

"If there's equality then the problem is solved. Because it is the corrupting power/inequality and its dividing of society into cliques vs the rest of us… and its inextricably linked distorting propaganda that is the poisonous problem."

"But that propaganda is weakening." replies Robert.

"Yes, definitely. Only about 10% of Brits get their news from the print rags. They are now weak. Thus it's already game over for them. They exist but in an innocent way… in a way equating to no real power. The decline of the press means the propaganda arm of the State is seen through."

Robert thinks for a moment about what he has just heard and then says…

"If that's anywhere near to true, then oh thank God! Because when you think about it, they are doing political gymnastics to look like they are doing nothing wrong. So take a right wing rag. They say they are for freedom of speech. Yet as Peter Oborne says about the Mail, they wouldn't allow him to criticise the paper in the Mail. So you ask, is that freedom of speech? Nah it's not. They are for freedom of speech where it suits. They are part-and-parcel of the Propaganda Matrix. They cancel speech that is critical of themselves. Of course they are ok with freedom of speech where it suits their agenda. But think about it… who isn't for freedom of speech that suits their own agenda? The test for freedom of speech is if they are for freedom of speech that is critical of their agenda. And on that score, the entire UK national Print Press fails."

"Yeah, they are for making themselves look good at all times."

"Exactly. And that requires Omissions Propaganda as well. That means omit the voices of different ideas. So for example, the fact that Brits are anti the State is something they would never discuss especially if it includes themselves. Could you imagine reading in the Mail or the Sun about a YouGov study into the British peoples attitudes to the Mail and the Sun."

"No I couldn't imagine it. And with good reason. Those studies have been carried out and they refuse to say a word on it."

"Omissions Propaganda."

"So they cancel criticism. They are agenda setting zealots. And they do omissions propaganda."

"Yes. And linked to agenda setting, the right wing rags do divide and rule."

"Basically, on the contrary to doing free speech, they do propaganda."

"Nailed it! They are obsessed with power and control. And that is what Peter Oborne says. He says that are not for freedom of speech but for control of speech. So lets think about that. They do not allow any criticism of themselves to be reported in their papers. And what they do allow in has to be consistent with their narrow political perspective. That's their omissions propaganda. So its not that they just deny criticism of themselves to be printed. Its more fair to say they do not allow the majority of thought to be expressed in their papers. But it gets worse. Their agenda setting is linked to divide and rule. Its not about supporting everyone. Far from it. They are basically vile."

Barry is drinking fast as the nerves of constant Chelsea possession in the cup match gets to him. He is constantly checking his watch.

Robert says

"We have to learn from their 24/7, 365 days a year deliberate mistakes. Anyone who is on our side who is like that is… NOT on our side at all. The Propaganda Matrix in terms of their right wing rags possess no self-criticism, no humility, no confession of hypocrisy because they care about power and control more than all of those things put together. No way can we allow ourselves to be the flip side of the same filthy coin."

"Well what you say about our side not being like that… I will drink to that. We must never go so low."

Middlesbrough win the first leg of the semi final Carabo Cup match 1–0. The three meet up again 2 weeks later on the night of the second leg. The location, as before is The Turners Mill.

2. Revolutionary Talk

"Not sure we can win this" says Barry who remembers all the possession Chelsea had in the first leg. He is also well aware that Chelsea beat Preston 4–0 in the FA Cup and they are only one place behind Boro in the league table.

"Well we are more interested in winning the analogous World Cup Final for the people" replies Robert who can't wait to get chatting like last time with Sally. They are all in their 30s and Robert's empathy with Sally means that Barry think there's an unspoken attraction between the two.

Sally sits down at the table with 3 drinks. Not all for herself! She says…

"We need to learn from the Propaganda Matrix' past success. What they have done so well for over 150 years is non-stop agenda setting. Their divide and rule agenda setting is of course, disgraceful. But it is highly successful. Obviously I don't mean we do divide & rule. But we do NOT allow the Propaganda Matrix to set the agenda. Hence, 24/7, 365 days a year of another agenda that is oblivious to what the Propaganda Matrix are dishing out. We establish two different worlds… their Propaganda State and our Non-Propaganda State."

"I see you notice what has happened. Those terms are now being used" replies Robert who is pleasantly surprised that a couple of terms he has long used such as Propaganda Matrix and Propaganda State are now being used by the masses.

"Yes. Everything is going our way."

"Therefore the Propaganda Matrix are no longer successful. Its like the People vs the State."

"Yup! In the past a political party that wanted to win could easily do so just by staying very close to the Status Quo. They didn't have to change anything hence it was nice and easy for them. There was a majority among the public that were for the status quo... or easy enough to be manipulated into being so. But all of that has changed. It is now being for the status quo that fails."

"So why is Starmer destined to be Prime Minister?"

"Because some of the public are still in the old fashioned way of looking at things… that if they just kick the other lot out then change happens. But most people now know that is total bullshit on stilts. But yes, the Tories are being blamed for the status quo. In reality ALL of the Propaganda Matrix are to blame… and that includes Labour. In reality its the People vs the State. It is not Labour vs Tory. The silly Labour vs Tory game is what the Propaganda Matrix tell you to think like. We MUST never again start dancing everytime we hear the Propaganda Matrix' tune. Life is not a peak time ITV Stage hypnosis entertainment show."

"People should have got here quicker… 40 years ago. Its been 40 years wasted."

"That is what you hear said all the time now. People look back 40 years and look at the garbage being spewed out by the likes of the Sun Newspaper which is now thought of as something that can only be defined using expletitives and people wonder… what were we thinking???"

Chelsea score and Barry is already certain of defeat even though its only 1–1 on aggregate. He decides to join in the political discussion.

"Right. If the present day people were transported back to the early 1990s the Sun would be laughed out of town. Now in 2024 the State requires consent from its people. That consent has to be close to the Status Quo. The consent needs to be in the Status Quo's circle or box. But people are now OUTSIDE of that box. And the State are thinking… GET BACK IN YOUR BOX!!! But people are not sheep. We cannot just be herded. People are refusing to get back in the box and are fighting back. We have grown a spine at last. If the metaphorical weather for the State used to be abit damp and abit miserable… now its a non-stop hurricane."

"GOOD!" replies Robert.

"Too many people for the Propaganda Matrix' liking are playing their game back at them! People have realized, like we have, how the Propaganda Matrix functions. It functions with non-stop agenda setting. They manufacture problems when in reality THEY ARE THE PROBLEM. So we see them going on about solving problems when as said, THEY ARE THE PROBLEM. Hence, they deflect from themselves and ask us to consume and validate their billionaire owned Cartel. They ask us to do this so they can solve the problems. When THEY ARE THE PROBLEM!!!" says Barry. He is saying what he thinks but he is also projecting abit of his frustration from the football match onto this other issue.

"People do not know how to bring the shitshow down. Although that is increasingly not true. But that 24/7, 365 days a year agenda setting they do, is now back in their face. Because people are seeing through the Propaganda Matrix. We have got them by the balls and the grip is getting tighter and tighter and tighter and tighter. The Status Quo State is going to fall!!!" says Sally.

"YASSS!!! I will drink to that!!!" replies Robert who continues…

"We give back what they dish out with interest!!!"

"33 cheers to that!"

"The Propaganda Matrix do not know how how to deal with this profound dislike they endure!"

"They could just f**k off!" says Barry. His two friends both respond with a simultaneous

"I wish!"

They laugh at the fact that their minds had thought so identically alike. But Barry isn't laughing as Chelsea go 2–1 ahead in the 2nd leg. Barry goes to the toilet partly so that he can get away from the match that he is NOT enjoying.

"What do you think is the key reason if you could only pick one policy why the Status Quo State is collapsing?" asks Sally. Robert answers…

"Housing costs! It means that people in their late 30s are still left wing focusing on social conditions as opposed to thinking about their kitchen's condition. There is a huge gulf between people in their late 30s now and those in their late 30s in the 1990s."

"Yes, so that could be viewed as linking to Universal Basic Income."

"It can be linked. But not necessarily. You could make housing affordable by making a lot of housing free."

"Or a mix of the two."

"Indeed. But anyway that is the answer. So if you want the State to collapse then you have to applaud the State for royally screwing up, knowing they have screwed up, yet they still don't correct their screw up."

"And of course there is the fact that people are becoming more educated. An educated society is impossible to govern."

"There is seemingly a statistical connection in modern societies between supporting the left wing and being more educated (probably more informed). There is also seemingly a statistical connection between having a bigger income and voting right wing. Tory PM's are educated outliers but are rightists due to high incomes."

"I see. So with Britons becoming simultaneously more educated and more poor it is a catastrophic cocktail for the Propaganda Matrix."

"Exactly. Our remote, clique Westminster SW1 cartel is becoming more and more of a remote, clique Westminster SW1 cartel, split off from the rest of society."

"Yes, because split off is a perception. You can't measure it and say NOW you are split off because the line is here and you have just gone over it. But the perception is that the Westminster political class are split off from society just like multi millionaires and billionaires are perceived by the public as being split off from society."

"We need a massive redistribution of power, wealth and income."

"Too right. 84% of Brits support a redistribution of income" says Rob showing his friend an online link to a study.

Barry returns and he says to go to the other part of the Turners Mill as he doesn't want to watch anymore of the football. While he was in the toilets Chelsea scored a third goal. Its now 3–0 on the night, 3–1 on aggregate. Liverpool or Fulham look like they will be playing Chelsea in the final. Liverpool and Fulham play tomorrow night.

Sally says

"I think the answer is to make everything 'small'. The News Media and even the pop culture world of movies, music and football. Power corrupts so don't allow for excess power to get a foothold. Don't allow for anything that looks empire-like, don't allow for anything that looks monopolistic. Even if they aren't literally empires or monopolistic… if they are being given those nicknames its because they are too big. We need to tackle all of that with these People's Courts that are starting to be created."

Robert responds

"Wow! Can you imagine how the British Propaganda Matrix is going to respond to those People's Courts. I'm not sure that we shouldn't do this through the Constitution rather than disowning Parliament and Downing Street completely. But the end of the sewer press will be a dream come true. Over a century of shit spewed out daily!"

"Hmmm… on the point about how will the State respond… obviously with violence!"

"So that will not be the propaganda side of the Propaganda Matrix being on display. It will be more a case of… the Propaganda Matrix' cover is blown so they just come out as the violent organisation that they always have been, are, and always will be. You see violence is not propaganda. Its what they dish out when the propaganda has been seen through."

"Yes. But that always will be isn't for much longer if their State collapses as it looks like is going to happen."

"The People's Courts, assuming they don't get smashed up by the Propaganda State, will do something substantial with Housing and the Cost of Living."

"Yup. And thank goodness for that! I may be sceptical about Peoples Courts but nothing is as bad as what we have now other than Nazi's gassing us all and nuclear holocaust."

"The Propaganda Matrix failed. They are a failed Propagandist State. They failed on wealth distribution, income distribution and power distribution." says Sally.

"Indeed, and the Failure is by design" replies Barry who despite having made his friends move to the other room in the Turners Mill in order to avoid watching the match, goes for a sneaky view at the screen.

Its now Chelsea 4–0 Middlesbrough and its not yet half time.

"Class war has become People's War." declares Robert.

"That is true! That links back to Brits becoming more and more educated and Brits becoming more and more poor" replies Sally.

These are an empathic trio on issues of power and inequality. But that is because they are all educated and all possess working class backgrounds.

"And really its not about Tory vs Labour with the people. When they get together you see that goes out of the window." Robert again shows his friends a study that demonstrates this fact.

Robert, while sceptical of People's Courts… he is nevertheless confident that more direct democracy can work. He says "To those who think that Brits coming together in something like a court system would not work at all, I recommend checking this out. First of all the key takeaway extract in italics is taken from the article linked to below it. Check out the article as well as the key take away extract."

"Kaela Scott, Design and Facilitation Lead for the Citizens' Assembly on Democracy in the UK and Direction of Innovation and Practice at Involve, added: "The recommendations from the Citizens' Assembly show that when members of the public are given the opportunity to come together and learn about the complexities of our democratic system, and the time to really discuss and deliberate on the system and what they want from it, they

can, despite their diversity, reach high levels of
agreement."

Landmark report shows UK citizens are 'deeply concerned' about their democracy | UCL News — UCL — University College London

Barry says "In all of this context, just think how people now think about things like the Post PM lecture circuit making them multi millionaires AND Murdoch News Media Empire."

"That latter one has crazily existed all of our life!" says the 37 year old Sally. Robert goes to the bar.

"Yeah and the People's Courts are being labelled Commie by the Propaganda Matrix. Even as they die they still dish out propaganda bullshit"

"Couldn't be more stupid given the people they are calling commie are now everyone!"

"So obvious that most of the British people are not commies. I mean its insane to think that Brits would get rid of the market in non-essentials. We don't even understand communism!"

"Exactly! The market is the best way to distribute goods over a wide area. But its more than that. If you mean communism like we saw in the 20th century then I accuse those communist regimes of being Propaganda Matrix'. I am anti dictatorial rule. The redistribution of power is key. If you give an individual dictatorial power then it corrupts that individual. We see the corruption in our Propaganda Matrix. And we observed that corruption in the Soviet Union. The Soviet Union had the Pravda newspaper mouthpiece of the government. We have the Murdoch Empire and the Mail. I support making a Guy Fawkes bonfire of all that criminalistic trash irrespective of whether its British, Russian or anything else."

Barry goes to the pubs toilets again partly to console himself over the football… Robert, who has returned with drinks starts scribbling some notes. He's writing a lot so it takes some time. When Barry returns he has still not finished scribbling away. Eventually he is able to show the notes to Barry and Sally.

Fair distribution of POWER) The people are humans thus corruptible. So to convince me that they would distribute power fairly (as opposed to doing a power grabbing takeover of the Propaganda Matrix) they would have to do something more than just say 'Trust me Bro'! Putting together a written constitution would suffice. If we are going to do People's Courts then The People's Courts would be loyal to the written constitution… not loyal to anything else.

Fair distribution of WEALTH and INCOME) Yes but don't destroy the market in non-essentials. As said the market is the best way of distributing goods over a wide area. On income distribution the way to convince me is again by guaranteeing a social democracy in the Constitution. (Generous minimum levels of income as a percentage of average overall incomes). Minimum acceptable for health policies on Housing, Health and Education would also be guaranteed in the Constitution. The Supreme Court would uphold these minimum standards and be able to go further if necessary.

Q) And what about the issue of violence (as in… a violent revolution)?

A) The first thing to say here is that you don't just try and bring down the State on any given day. In other words you don't wake up on Tuesday morning and say "No time like the present!" We would be destroyed like bugs. What you do is first and foremost ensure that the State has almost completely lost the support of the people. In other words, its parties would be all finished and its news media would be hated like Nazi-esque propaganda. You also ensure that the people know what the alternative is. So rather like the army is the last resort for the State… our violence is also very last resort. We aim to peel off people within the State (including the violent part of the state) to get them onto our side. We would just send some of our toughest people out to finish the almost dead State off with violence. They would be arrested. They would be treated very well and we would give them their freedom back when the State had entirely lost. The only reason we would arrest them in the first place is to stop them harming us. (It would be self-defence). We would just be stopping them playing silly games. It would have been Game Over for themselves ages ago. No more Propaganda Matrix so why would they still be fighting us? But there's always some who would, as Hitler did, fight when it would only make things worse for their own side.

Barry has a good read and then says…

"That is what is happening right now!"

"I know. The amazing thing is NOT that people have seen through. We have got used to that. What is amazing is that they are acting on it."

"Yeah and we are part of the people so I suppose its not too surprising that you and me agree with exactly what is happening."

"Well, they haven't won yet and penned a Constitution so I suppose it could go pear shaped" says Sally.

"It brilliantly AUTHENTIC. Not playing the fake anti establishment game. We really are anti establishment. Our movement truly exists outside of the Propaganda Matrix and we simply need to make ourselves organized and visible. I am 100% supportive. This is what PEOPLE'S WAR looks like!" says Barry.

"I penned this yesterday on my Medium Page" Rob says showing Barry and Sally his example of how the Propaganda Matrix does divide and rule.

Example of Propaganda Matrix Divide and Rule

Victorian England started the Propaganda Matrix as we know it with the introduction of the Print Press. Right from the start they poured poison into peoples minds. A book could be written on it. The huge news story concerning Victorian England occurred in 1888 when Jack the Ripper murdered and mutilated the bodies of multiple women. The newly formed British Print Press cried out A Jew must have done it! That is crystal clear divide and rule propaganda. The same print press also argued that no Englishman would do such a thing. (as if Jews can't also be English!) So just imagine if Jack the Ripper had been caught and that he was a Jew. The right wing press would have shouted from the rooftops… told you so! Typical Jew!

They would have made out that Jews are like that and it validates their view they had articulated, that it must be a Jew doing this. Meanwhile, had an Englishman (who was not a Jew) been discovered to have been Jack the Ripper... well then the press would have just said... well this has nothing to do with the fact that he is English. Its just a one-off madman!

The UK's Victorian Press demonstrates that the UK's propaganda rags have always done divide and rule. If there had been no Jews in London at the time, but had been a significant minority of Italians instead then the press would have gone after the Italians.

These anti Jew sentiments continued to exist after 1888... its just that from our time in the 2020s the Jack the Ripper story stands out a mile. So imagine being born into that climate. We can take 1888 as a year of birth for X. Then X would be 35 years old in 1923. Or we can just go a fraction into the future (from 1888's perspective) and take 1896 as a year of birth. Because that is when Oswald

Mosley was born. Mosley was born 7 miles away from Whitechapel. Whitechapel was where Jack the Ripper did his killings so the anti Jewish attitude was something he was born into. By the 1920s and 1930s Mosely had quite a following. He even got to visit Hitler in Germany so that implies that Mosley was making enough waves in the UK for the German Nazi Party leader to notice him. You could say that Mosley's Fascist Party had become the sister party of Hitler's Nazi's. Of course, in Germany too, the Nazi Party of Hitler, Himmler, Hess etc… had similarly been born into a culture that was prejudice towards Jews. In the 1920s these anti-semite future German leaders were gangsters shooting at Police in the streets. That ended up with a prison sentence for Hitler where he penned Mein Kampf. I can safely say I have never read it but I hear it is riddled with hate on every page, especially for Jews. The point I am wanting to make is this… The late Victorian AND early 20th century Propaganda Matrix in England and Germany brought about Mosley and Hitler… and their supporters. Hence the Propaganda Matrix gaslit the public and then walked away playing the innocent. That had worse consequences for Germany than the UK, resulting in the extermination of millions of Jews. While it also required the Wall Street Crash to bring the Nazi's to power, they used the anti Jewish propaganda that they were familiar with in order to give them an edge over other right wing parties. Hence, the German Nazi's couldn't have achieved power without the earlier in time anti Jewish propaganda. The German Propaganda Matrix enabled Gangsters to take over the Propaganda Matrix. It could have happened in the UK. This anti semitism example is an excellent example of the Propaganda Matrix' divide and rule. The Propaganda Matrix do it for their own benefit but the more success they attain the more they empower extremist groups that civilized society stays well clear of because they are hooligans or gangsters who should be in prison as opposed to being in power. Our present day Propaganda Matrix do divide and rule.

"It just shows how important it is to NOT allow the UK's Propaganda Matrix to set the agenda. The people must isolate the clique and then the clique will melt into civilization anyway and we would finally experience a

People's society as opposed to a clique ruling for themselves and multi millionaires/billionaires" says Barry *who then hears someone say that Chelsea are winning 6–0. He then goes outside for some fresh air.*

"We need to peel off people within the Propaganda Matrix getting them to disown it" says Robert.

"That would mean we win over figures within their billionaire owned news media to come over to our news media… which would always be deliberately kept small so as not to become corrupted. It would mean winning over politicians (not yet corrupted) to our side. They would be giving up on corrupting power by doing so as we do not go in for the grandiosity of Parliament etc. You are just a person like the rest of us. We would already have the academic world and scientists. They would be tasked with getting the People's Courts up-and-running. This would mean people in the army coming over to our side. They would hopefully never be required but you can imagine the Propaganda Matrix wanting to injure and kill us… so it would help to win the army over to our side as preferable to the army acting threatening and violent towards us. We also want to win over the Police. If you don't give a crap about symbolism then I am 100% fine with that. But if you do like symbolism then how about this… the Written Constitution would be penned in Liverpool. We are from the northeast. We don't support Liverpool FC or Everton, but Liverpool have suffered a-lot at the hands of the Propaganda Matrix… hence it would be a nice symbolic touch to write the Constitution in Liverpool" argues Sally, who, to be honest, is happily going along with quite alot of what she has heard suggested. The Peoples Courts and the Liverpool idea are all expected to occur.

Robert responds

"We need to get 20 or 30 academics/Policemen/Policewomen/Army members/reporters together… preferably (but not necessarily) in Liverpool… use our own news media… and then introduce this movement to the British public.

Then more join this noble project. We get the numbers. We ignore the Propaganda Matrix. Once we have the required number of people in place… we start up the People's Courts and take it from there." says Robert, still with doubt in his mind about the People's Courts but easily preferring the idea to the status quo.

Barry comes back but only to say goodbye for the night as he is dissillusioned about the football. He misses a consolation goal for Middlesbrough but that only means it finished Chelsea 6–1 Middlesbrough on the night… 6–2 on aggregate. Chelsea will play Liverpool or Fulham in the Final.

"What I wonder is why do you think the Propaganda Matrix are dying?" asks Sally.

"It's partly or largely due to the changed news media landscape. Only 10% maximum get their news from print newspapers. Now let's say that 7% of that news media is right wing, well most people who read the right wing press are NOT voting Tory anymore. While some of them are voting Reform UK more than 50% of right wing newspapers are voting for parties that are perceived to be left of centre. Hence of the 7% reading right wing print newspapers with most of them not voting Tory we can say that only 3 out of 100 Brits are arguably publicly influenced by right wing print press."

"And yet they still largely set the agenda the cheeky sods" responds Sally.

"True. But that's unsustainable."

"There's GB News."

"Ok. Take the 3 in every 100 up to 4 in 100 maximum."

"But we are not for the Propaganda Matrix once the Tories are extinct."

"True. The Propaganda Matrix means much more than a few right wing rags that everyone has seen through."

"We have to destroy Starmer's Labour Party. They are a Cameron style Tory Party."

"And have you noticed that the Reform UK Party are supported by a whole load of people who support a redistribution of power, wealth and income? Yet their leader, Tice, would probably vanquish the welfare state and privatise the NHS given half a chance."

"Now that's an example of Propaganda Matrix scoring success. They take a bunch of people as their supporters who are therefore our opponents, but its only because they are successfully manipulated by propaganda."

"We have to unite. That's the point. With the propaganda State's power getting weaker and weaker it will become impossible for them to manipulate. We then have to unite."

"You know what would be best for peace?"

"What would be best for peace?"

"The U.S. Democrats getting a mauling. Everyone else over there seems to be anti war."

"Yeah. Britain doesn't go into any major wars without protection from the U.S."

"The Propaganda Matrix doesn't want to get its ass kicked!"

"Good. Because they would take us down with them if they didn't mind getting a sore ass from Johnny foreigner playing a one-sided football match with it."

It is lucky Barry wasn't still here otherwise he might have felt like that was a dig at him given the one-sided football match that had gone against his side.

"Britain's war mongering is fake given that it always wants to be protected as a puppet of the U.S."

"Yeah. At least people get that U.S. thing."

"No war other than class war!!!"

"YASSS!"

"That counts for both the candy floss culture war and the psychopathic nuclear holocaust war."

"Exactly. Our war is about money or bread as people say."

"Housing and money."

"Yeah, its a-bit more than that. But basically that's the end goal."

"The means to get there is the strategy. We have to take down the Propaganda State because they endlessly deflect onto other issues so as to divide us. Yet all we are asking for is bread."

"Well the good news is they have relatively lost their megaphones. They are weaker than we are now. Without their megaphones that they once possessed far more people listen and empathise with what we say and think. No one listens to them anymore" says Sally.

"I largely agree. People say all the things we say. They just haven't put it all together because they aren't as obsessed as we are."

"Anyone who thinks what we are saying is unrealistic needs to hear the following... In both France and Germany their traditional major parties are either tiny now or basically extinct because they can't even win enough votes to make the 5% vote share to get back their deposit. They fail to get 5% in their elections. That's because of the demise of their Propaganda States."

"For them, like for us, they can unite now. They just have to do it. It's an open goal."

"Right. So in the UK with millions of people unable to get housing to live independently and with people on Universal Credit being about £6,000 a year short of being able to cover the cost of heating and eating, there's an inability of the Propaganda Matrix to be able to justify it. The people who say it like it is (i.e., its an injustice!) win the argument everytime. Any attempt to justify it sounds ridiculous."

"The Propaganda Matrix looks so f*****g stupid!"

"That's because they are so f*****g stupid!"

"We are kicking their ass!"

"Good. Let's kick it harder until its as sore as if a Lion had took a bite out of it."

"We need the lion to eat that ass!"

"So the Tories go the of the German and French parties and then we transform Labour. It becomes a new animal... we become that animal. And we get money and housing to ourselves."

"Yeah, and with the Propaganda Matrix dead in the water, we get beyond the propaganda. So for example, the Propaganda Matrix is already dead in the water on money issues."

"Yes. That is clear in the sense that the public put the cost of living crisis as the number 1 issue they want solving. Thus the Propaganda Matrix has failed to protect itself in this crucial area. You could imagine their desire for the people to blame themselves for their own hardship."

"Yeah, this really gets across the Propaganda State's demise."

"They are seen through!"

"So we need to get together with those who are sometimes deemed to be our enemies but who are not our enemies. Because the working class per se has seen through this shit show."

"Overcome the fake division."

"Ignore the cartel at Westminster and support getting housing and money to people."

"Yeah… and stop allowing the cartel to say, hey, this time we have got the right man or woman for you lot to support."

"Ha Ha Ha. I think when the Tories did that one every few months or every few weeks, they did better than we could in getting the message across that you would have to be a dumb ass to ever fall for that nonsense ever again."

3. Civil War

People's Courts are being established throughout the UK. Or to put it more precisely, people are trying to establish People's Courts throughout the UK. This project is organised by academics, business people, trade unionists, people working within the sciences, and people working within the arts. However, there is a serious problem. That problem is that the Police keep piling in and trashing the People's Courts. And there is a pattern that is easy to observe. Each time the Court gets smashed to pieces, some of the organisers get arrested while others who escape the police's detection go outside and complain to news media about the disrespect. The Police violence and arrests then fuels anger among the people and they react with violence of their own. Therefore it looks like Britain is spiralling towards civil war. The Police hit back by saying that although it looks to some people like they were the cause of the increased violence in society, the courts are illegal so what are they to do? The people respond that the State has been seen through and no longer has the people's consent so what are they. the people, supposed to do.

The Propaganda State has had its turn. Pollsters demonstrate that most of the public are on the side of the Non-Propaganda State. Indeed if they were not, then the fight would be pointless. The politicians reaction is to spit their dummy out and verbally lash out at the people. Meanwhile the Mail, Sun, Express and Telegraph lead with silly lecturing front page headlines such as 'WHY WON'T THEY ARREST THEM?' The police are making arrests but it is hard to arrest millions of people. The readers of those propaganda rags overwhelmingly support the Non-Propaganda State. And they cease to purchase the Propagandist State Rags with sales plummeting close to zero. The national print press is in its final weeks of existence. And they are within a whisker of going out of business following headlines that repeatedly lash out at the People following the Great Revolutionary Riot of 27 February 2024.

The riot occurred unsurprisingly at the location of Westminster SW1. A staggering 4 million people turned up to block access to Downing Street, and Parliament. This resulted in running battles with the Police as the people reacted to the attack by launching their own attack. Water canons were used, batons were used, German Shepherd dogs were used. The police had shields but the sheer number of people they were up against guaranteed days of fighting. There wasn't a politician in sight at Westminster and the news media were frightened to be there as well but most did turn up at their own risk.

Outside of the UK, governments such as those in the U.S., Australia, Canada and throughout Western Europe sided with the UK's Propaganda State. However, this was uncomfortable for them as the UK's government was confessing that they will govern as a dictatorship. They used the bizarre excuse of having no choice. But they did have a choice as they had lost public consent. They could have just cleared off. The British people felt like they were taking on the world with no friends outside of the UK. But this isn't true. Many people in other nations were supporting the people. So for example a slight majority of American, Canadian and Australians were on the British publics side. And a clear majority of French people were on the British publics side presuambly because the French admire revolutionaries due to their own history.

Domestically, the political parties had been exposed as a key ingredient of the Propaganda Matrix. The Labour and Tory Parties were united in an attempt to create a feeling of national unity against the enemy within. But they had been well and truly seen through. Only the Green Party rejected the Propaganda Matrix. They officially ended their party and joined the public as individuals following the Labour and Tory parties call for the army to fight the people to the death. The threat of the army did frighten some of the people to cease fighting. The army itself was worried about causing a massacre of its own people and it secretly requested talks with the now dying and in-hiding so-called national government. But vocally, Labour and Tory voices kept shouting on the TV news… shouting things like 'Arrest them' and 'Fight them'. Most Britons were not being violent at all. Of course, it is difficult to be a peaceful pacifist when the Propaganda Matrix are sending out their violent upholders of the Propaganda Matrix to do their dirty work for them. Naturally, supporters of the Non-Propaganda Matrix kept saying that if the Propaganda Matrix just accepted its death then Britain would be at peace again. But that was not the direction of travel in late February and the start of March 2024. With about 85% of Britons supporting the Non-Propaganda Matrix the police were no longer considered effective enough to win a civil war against the people. And therefore the weak national government tried to assert dictatorial strength as it managed to persuade the British army to defeat the British people.

4. Liverpool

The location is St Georges Hall in the heart of Liverpool City Centre. Delegates and Representatives are there to draft the new Non-Propaganda States constitution. Legal experts are in attendance as well as leading academics from across the United Kingdom. Some national news media networks are also here but not all as some are protesting at being labeled Propagandist by the emerging Non-Propagandist State. Thousands of people are outside the building, 99% of which are fully supportive. Huge cheers went up when the delegates arrived at St Georges. They were indeed greeted like pop stars. Speaking of stars from the world of music, it is Paul McCartney that is about to come to the podium to welcome everyone to this proud and historic event. But just as he is about to be introduced a number of people inside the building hear commotion coming from outside. The Army had turned up and fighting had broke out as the people tried to prevent the army storming the building. It was absolute mayhem. And then the unthinkable happened. Shots were fired.

Screaming and total chaos ensured. People were lying on the ground injured, dying or dead. Not surprisingly this enabled the army to break through and enter the building. They went on to trash the place, reminscent of what happened in Catalonia when Catalonians tried for independence. They stormed the inside of the building hitting anyone who got in their way with batons. McCartney himself was smashed in the face, his face visibly injured with bruising. This tragedy in Liverpool is much worse than the scenes seen in Catalonia years earlier. Again Liverpool is a victim of the State… with 5 innocent people murdered.

The news spreads like wildfire. Sky News never turned up to the St Georges Hall event. Nevertheless within a few minutes of the drama Kay Burley (Sky News) reports on the Breaking News:

"We are hearing that 5 people have been killed while trying to defend St Georges Hall in Liverpool where the Written Constitution was set to be signed and presented to delegates and representatives. The news that is just coming through to us is that the British Army turned up and opened fire on people outside the building. Right, in my ear I am being told that we now have footage of what happened from other news media that were there. Given what we know of what happened we advise that what you about to see will be very distressing. So if you are still watching I warn you that these pictures I suspect will show people being killed."

The footage does indeed show murders taking place, two of which were clear to see.

Back in Liverpool those who had attended the event walk out of St Georges and sought out news media. Tina Walker, a Politics Tutor from the University of Manchester made sure she found supportive press that would quote what she says. Hence she walked past the dying national news media and after a few minutes, found reporters from the Liverpool Echo. The echo reporters had brought a television camera with them. As soon as they were rolling Walker shouted

"Murdering Bastards!"

"The State has declared war on the public! That means a civil war!"

"Scum!"

That is all she had to say. Her blood is boiling. But the following day the Echo lead with Walkers words: MURDERING BASTARDS!

A split emerges between national and local newspapers. There's also a split between national and local TV News with the locals in both cases supporting the people's Non-Propagandist State. The nationals on the other hand are supporting the old Propagandist State. The scenes that people see on their TV and online social media screens result in the worst riots ever seen in known history in the United Kingdom. Cities (and towns) become war-zones. But the interesting point here is that it is not a simple case of People vs Police. It looks like it is. Until it becomes clear that many of the Police are fighting with the people against the Police. This makes the outcome less clear especially when it is further realized that most fireman have come out fighting with the people. Also the Army are not involved at all. They have ignored the Old Propaganda Matrix's outgoing Tory Government's order to fight the people. Instead they are considering where their loyalties lie. This is absolutely huge news. Should the army come out in favour of the Propaganda State then they could limp on for decades as some kind of hated dictatorship. But if they come out in favour of the people then its over for the Propaganda State.

If the Propaganda State were to win this civil war it would mean it effectively ruling over its own people with none of the pasts pretence about being a democracy. It had confessed (as it had no choice) to being a dictatorship. It had always been a dictatorship. It was only ever a democracy in name. But now it had dropped the label democracy. So this civil war is now openly a fight between the People for the People and Dictators for Dictators. The favourites to win up until 5.59pm on 9 March were the Dictators.

At 6pm on 9th March 2024 the UK's Chief of the General Staff, Peter Stevens, who had just taken over from Patrick Sanders who had quit minutes earlier, went on Live TV and issued a statement declaring the Army's support for the people. This instantly shifted the power dynamic in the UK from the Propagandist State to the Non Propagandist State effectively instantly ending the State as we know it.

5. Wild Celebrations and calm

As the news quickly filtered through to almost everyone, the majority of authorities fighting the people ceased to do so. Indeed they no longer had any authority. And the vast majority of people who were fighting for the Non-Propaganda State ceased fighting too… and instead engaged in wild celebrations.

The people ultimately wanted calm. The wild celebrations were due to the end of a Propaganda Matrix that ruled over people for its own benefit and thus manipulated the people in order to be able to do so. The national news media as we knew it no longer existed. Parliament and Downing Street were empty.

Equality is (and always was) the cure for the mental illness that is power politics. People looked back at the Propaganda Matrix as the same as a primary school playground in terms of is maturity. Because it was the case that power politics meant that its politicians and news media had demonstrated anti social, mentally undeveloped attitudes for well over a century.

The people were not utopians. Rather think of the Non-Propaganda State as analogous to the field of medical science. Medical science isn't a utopian field. It is simply mature. And as the Constitution and the Peoples Court's combined to bring about UBI and a sizeable sector of free housing, well then the celebrations died down and the contentment and calm became the norm. The increase in people in their 30s and 40s living independently sky rocketed… too many had been relying on their elderly parents under the Propaganda Matrix. Free housing combined with UBI also sorted out the cost of living crisis. Hence it was contentment that people felt. They did not feel wildly celebratory. The wild celebration was about what was being destroyed more than it was what would be gained… although it was both. All that is meant here is that the former was deemed essential for sanity. Once people were simply treating themselves with respect it became taken for granted. People looked back bemused at how it was we ever let it be so different. So it was rather like medical science or law courts that have always existed. In other words the Non-Propaganda State is not the drama queen that the Propaganda State was.

Brits now live in peace and equality. There was a counter revolution attempt by billionaire funded milita and gangsters but the British Army overpowered them easily and speedily. The counter revolution attempt was over in less than a week.

Unfortunately there was one organisation that wasn't playing fair.

6. A Quiet Counter Revolution

A quiet counter revolution indeed is a-foot. The people had seemingly defeated power grabbers but one institution had been overlooked. That institution was the British Civil Service. This was something that Redcar's Robert Sutton had wondered about. But many had clearly not wondered enough about it. The Civil Service did not mind the progressive policy initiatives that they had to implement. But they sensed that the Non-Propaganda State had effectively assumed that the civil service would innocently play along with the new reality. But the civil service is not, and never has been, as innocent as it looks. Prime Ministers (from Thatcher to Blair) said that the civil service likes things done a certain centrist way. It likes to be in control and prefers the familiar. The civil service, they and others said) always regarded Prime Ministers and Government as here today and gone tomorrow, whereas they the civil service, are permanent. Thus so the logic goes, the civil service regarded themselves as the most important player because permanent beats temporary.

My word, how the Non-Propagandists underestimated the civil service. The top of the Civil Service considered themselves to be now navigating uncharted territory. This is not to say that everyone within the civil service reacted in the same way. However not many top civil servants went along with the language of Propaganda and Non-Propaganda State. Some referred to the People's revolution. Some unkindly referred to the Plebs Revolution. Some officials embraced the new reality and worked diligently to support the directives of the People's Courts, recognizing them as the legitimate governing body. Others to put it politely harbored reservations about this abrupt change and sought ways to ensure that governance remains stable and effective during this period of transition. However, others (and these were the very top of the civil service) regarded the Plebs Revolution as a national disgrace and an insult. They viewed it as an attack on institutional integrity and as Britain being defeated in a World War. At first the British people did not realize the Civil Service possessed these attitudes. The focus was never on the Civil Service. The focus was constantly on everyday people. Those tiny few who did think about the Civil Service simply thought they were carrying out the people's directives. Afterall the Civil Service had done precisely that. What the people did not know is that the Civil Service were plotting to such an extent that they would rightly be categorized as counter revolutionaries.

They wanted all kinds of things restored. They wanted links to other nations. They wanted Parliament restored. They wanted Downing Street restored. They wanted political parties restored. Basically they wanted the Propaganda Matrix restored. This equated to a serious threat to the Non-Propaganda Matrix. The Civil Service used its power and influence to infiltrate the legal profession that organised much of these Courts decisions on what policy initatives were to be decided on in the Court System. What the Civil Service were trying to do was to turn back the clock and reestablish what they preferred. In order to do this they had to take control of the Supreme Court as their goal was to get the issue of a return to (what they called) parliamentary democracy discussed in the Peoples Courts. The Civil Service thus used its experience to infiltrate law… and thus eventually, much to the people's horror won its quest for a Counter Revolution and restored what the people considered to be 'The Propaganda State' in the not very united… United Kingdom.

7. Oh how ironic!

What the Civil Service considered as Parliamentary Democracy… the British People now called 'Propaganda Matrix'. The Civil Service argued that they had implemented the policies of the People's Courts. However, this argument was rather weak as they could hardly be regarded as having respected the People's Courts now that they had vanquished them and also ended its Constitution. People noted the Civil Servants propagandist slant when they talked like that. Afterall the people didn't pretend to have been respectful to the Propaganda State when they had got rid of the Propaganda State. That would be propaganda if they had. Rather there had been wild celebrations.

The Non-Propaganda State (during its short spell of existence) had brought in Universal Basic Income and Free Housing. They had also ensured Britain was safe from war, and was thus at peace. And their Constitution had ensured that radical social democracy was to be as far to the right as the UK could go… and no limits were set concerning how far left. However, it was never expected that the market in non-essentials would be threatened. At least that was the spectrum in terms of Power, Wealth and Income distribution. There has also been a constitutional law stating that Britain's army only exists to defend Britain from invasion from the outside… and from enemies within. However, the Civil Service used their brain to get around that problem. Meaning that the Civil Service did not need the army on side as the Civil Service would use its brain rather than violence to get what it wanted. The Civil Service succeeded in a counter revolution without firing a single shot. Fair enough, Civil Servants aren't exactly violent but they sure were sly. And the result… a British population now more extreme than ever. And with the right wing news media, now more sewer-like than ever, back up and running, and the hate being spewed out all aimed at the defeated supporters of the Non-Propaganda State… well now there were far right fascists and Nazi's (who were not bothering to hide their political affiliations) who were hell bent on pursuing a Hitler style direction for the UK. But they were still the minority. So be grateful for small mercies. Those who supported a return to the Non-Propaganda State didn't quite know what to do. But then a new political party was created which openly appealed to that large political demographic. This new party was called the Democratic Socialist Party. It campaigned on:

Supporting the newly established UBI Policy.

Supporting the newly established Housing Policy.

Re-establishing the Socialist Constitution with the same minimum social democratic principles to be applied in the UK at all times on the issue of wealth and income. On power, no where should a monopoly emerge without being quashed. In other words, whether it be too much political power, too much power over an industry etc. So again, everything had to be small. A Prime Minister could not serve for long. (This was nicknamed 'The Liz Truss Principle'.) News Media had to be small so there was no chance of a Rupert Murdoch News Media Empire existing ever again. Letting the national news print press die off once-and-for-all. So their propaganda is eliminated forever. As before the Constitution also set out the role for Britain's defence as meaning what it says on the tin: i.e., defence. (not attack). Thus Britain would only defend itself if attacked from enemies without and enemies within.

On the basis that power corrupts, and on the basis of multimillionaires and billionaires ability to create near monopolies, they were to be taxed to the hilt. A Wealth Tax would be introduced. The Democratic Socialists were well aware that the super rich might pack their bags and move to a more right wing environment, well so-be-it.

Everywhere where excess power takes hold it would be come down upon like a ton of bricks.

The NHS would be supported with record spending year in-year out.

People pursuing higher education courses would be given top-up grants (i.e., top-up of their Universal Basic Income).

A market in non-essentials would remain in place and the Democratic Socialists would work with the Bank of England to ensure that there was no boom and bust and no high inflation as a consequence of these policies. And no scaring the markets.

Targeted subsidies of industries such as gas, electric and rail in order to make the UK among the lowest charges for these services in the world. Due to UBI the Democratic Socialists would not make those services free but they would be very low cost.

Society would no longer be the play thing of the super-rich and the old Propaganda Matrix. Its days of exploiting the people were well and truly over. The Democratic Socialists won the General Election and the new order, with its socialist constitution became the norm in the UK for as far ahead as one could possibly imagine.

8. Abroad

The French were rather surprised that the Brits had gone through revolutionary change before they themselves had done so. Nevertheless French radicals were unsurprisingly inspired and they had a new found fondness for the UK who they, as in the French people, now deemed as their Number 1 ally. Of course the French State viewed the initial People's Courts idea with horror and the French State in general disapproved of the new found British radicalism, especially what they perceived as being the UK's isolationism on military matters. The UK had withdrawn from NATO resulting in the French accusing the Brits of Trumpism. Nevertheless they had been expecting more British isolationism ever since Brexit. But they were primarily relieved that the Brits had pulled back on the abolition of Parliament and Downing St. Because if the Brits could get rid of their State then the French radicals and revolutionaries would have been inspired. Indeed they had been but at least now the UK's radicalism did not mean getting rid of its most obvious symbols of power, even if excess power was no longer a reality in the UK. The French Propaganda State could easily spin their way out of that argument being used against themselves. Abit of omissions propaganda could help in their quest.

France's civil war was different to what Britain's had been. In Britain it was the People vs the Propaganda State. And indeed, many French radicals tried for an exact copy of the original British experience. Unfortunately, too many French people had a taste for Marine Le Pen. And hence, the people split in two. On one side there were the majority of French who were fighting for a Non-Propaganda State. But there were 20–25% of the French population fighting for a Marine Le Pen dictatorship. Meanwhile the

Emmanuel Macron liberal centrist government fought both sides on the streets. Naturally the Parisian riots that ensued were described as the worst sustained violence since the French revolution of 1789 to 1799. But now in June 2024 disaster struck when the French Army split in three… some supporting Macron, some supporting Le Pen and some supporting the majority of the people. This resulted in months of violence with no side getting a clear upper hand. Eventually a truce was reached with the French Propaganda State remaining in place and with France broken up into Liberal territories and Far Right territories. But they kept fighting each other for years leading to France being constantly regarded as the classic example of an unstable nation and Failed State.

Much of Western Europe underwent major change. But only Switzerland went as far as the original British People's Courts idea. The other major nations (France as we have seen, and Italy and Germany) did not. Australia and Canada tried to bring in People's Courts. The Canadian people went head to head against their propaganda Matrix but lost when the Canadian army (supported with help from the United States) defeated the Canadian people. Many Canadians fled to the UK and to other western European nations that had Non-Propaganda States. The attempt of the Australians to copy the Brits went wrong when their Army opted to support the People but the people did NOT decentralise power to people's courts. They established a new Propaganda Matrix instead with a clique of people possessing vastly unequal power in their own favour. They took over the existing news media and justified it using all the old propagandist methods. Meanwhile the U.S. and Russian Propaganda Matrix' remained intact meaning that tensions continued to exist between those nations. The UK's Non-Propaganda State did not get involved in other nations affairs and therefore did not suffer from Cold War or hot war fears. In terms of the health of their people history would judge the UK to have come out best of all, at least in terms of the health and contentment of their people. Switzerland were second most successful but they suffered from terrorism… the terrorists being right wing crazies wishing to restore the old order. This attracted the type of person who wanted to play power politics all of the time. Overall Britain's radicalism ultimately worked for itself but caused chaos for other nations.

NOTES/CREDITS

SOUNDTRACK: Revolution by the Beatles.

The Mail
ON SUNDAY

JANUARY 21, 2024

£2.10 £1.80 to subscribers

With £10bn bonus in his kitty, Chancellor tells MoS he'll
emulate Treasury giant behind 1980s economic revival

HUNT: TAX CUTS WILL SPARK NEW LAWSON BOOM

EXCLUSIVE

By **Glen Owen** POLITICAL EDITOR

JEREMY HUNT has vowed to emulate Nigel Lawson, the tax-cutting Chancellor whose radical economic policies led to the Big Bang in financial markets and propelled Margaret Thatcher to a third Election win.

The Chancellor uses a gung-ho article in today's Mail on Sunday to hail the economic boom Lord Lawson created in the 1980s – and pledges to usher in his own version, starting with tax cuts in his Budget on March 6.

He says: 'The most dynamic economies tend to be places with lower taxes. The lesson is clear: supporting businesses with competitive taxes – not more government spending – is the way to growth.'

Mr Hunt's remarks came after the Financial Times reported that his hopes of being able to announce a tax-cutting bonanza were boosted by estimates that his headroom for cuts has increased by £10billion as a result of lower than expected Government borrowing

Turn to Page 8

ROYAL EXCLUSIVE

Harry's selfie with fake prince – but not a word for his sick dad

Pages 2-3

Search   Write

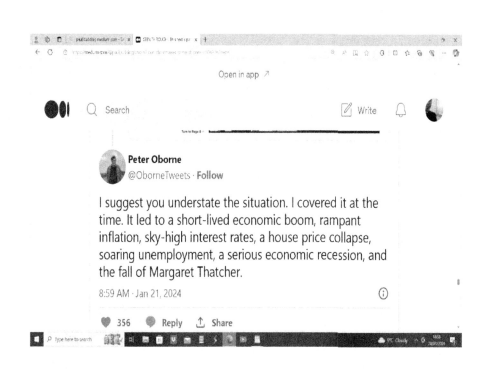

Peter Oborne
@OborneTweets · **Follow**

I suggest you understate the situation. I covered it at the
time. It led to a short-lived economic boom, rampant
inflation, sky-high interest rates, a house price collapse,
soaring unemployment, a serious economic recession, and
the fall of Margaret Thatcher.

8:59 AM · Jan 21, 2024   ⓘ

♥ 356   💬 Reply   ⬆ Share

Above: The Daily Mail supporting the budget that led to Liz Truss and Kwasi Kwarteng's resignations. Truss only

lasted as Prime Minister for 50 days. Kwarteng only lasted only 38 days as Chancellor.

Below: An example of delusional front page from a dying newspaper (The Express) talking to itself, not even talking the language of its own readers… report penned in late January 2024. I thought that it was worth including this front page headline in my book so that post-General Election 2024 the readers of my book will have a classic and obvious example of mind boggling bias and stupidity (delusional nonsense) from the dying print press.

SUNDAY ✠ EXPRESS

JANUARY 28, 2024   express.co.uk   £2.40

FREE FAMILY PASS £50 WITH THE 🍂 National Trust PAGE 32

EXCLUSIVE Grace killer was 'not insane' say experts PAGE 7

RISHI TARGETS SAGA VOTES TO WIN ELECTION

- **PM reaches out to the 26 million over-50s, saying 'I'm on your side'**

- **Shocking rise in middle-aged still struggling to get on housing ladder**

EXCLUSIVE

By David Williamson POLITICAL EDITOR

Smiling Queen's 3-hour hospital visit to King Charles
PAGE 5

TURN TO PAGE FOUR

Why the *above* headline is delusional. This sort of polling has been the consistent pattern for a couple of years.

Will Jennings 🦋
@drjennings · **Follow**

X

Voting intention by age tells a remarkable story about British politics.

18-24: Con 9, Lab 60, Ref 3
25-49: Con 14, Lab 57, Ref 8
50-64: Con 20, Lab 49, Ref 14
65+: Con 35, Lab 25, Ref 22

 **YouGov** ✓ @YouGov

Latest YouGov Westminster voting intention (23-24 Jan)

Con: 20% (no change from 16-17 Jan)
Lab: 47% (=)
Lib Dem: 8% (=)
Reform UK: 13% (+1)
Green: 6% (-1)
SNP: 4% (+1)

This is our highest figure for Reform UK to date

yougov.co.uk/politics/artic

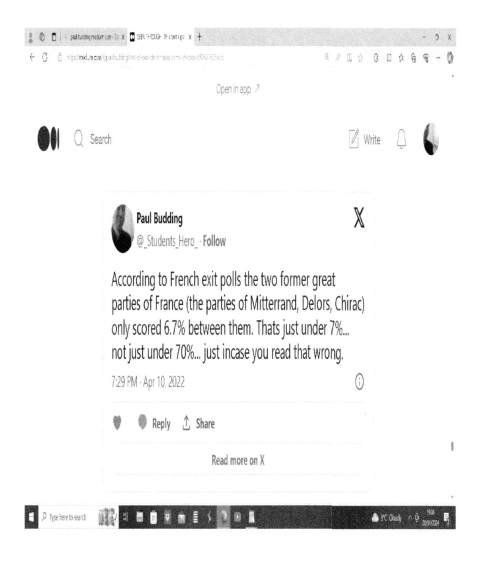

Paul Budding
@_Students_Hero_ · **Follow**

X

According to French exit polls the two former great parties of France (the parties of Mitterrand, Delors, Chirac) only scored 6.7% between them. Thats just under 7%... not just under 70%... just incase you read that wrong.

7:29 PM · Apr 10, 2022

Reply   ⬆ Share

Read more on X

Below: The Sun Newspaper style reporting on Hillsbrough that led to the sale of the Sun being banned in Liverpool.

THE Sun

Wednesday, April 19, 1989   20p   Yesterday's sale: 4,310,811   PRINTED IN THE NORTH

THE TRUTH

Tycoon Adnan thrown in jail

By SUN FOREIGN DESK

ARMS tycoon Adnan Khashoggi, once one of the world's richest men, was seized on massive fraud charges yesterday.

Police swooped in Switzerland after he flew in for "eternal youth" health treatment.

He was jailed awaiting a bid to extradite him to America, where an international warrant had been issued for him.

Khashoggi, 53, is accused of helping deposed Philippines president Ferdinand Marcos steal £100 MILLION from his country's treasury.

He could face 25 years jail if convicted in the US.

FBI investigators say Khashoggi pretended to be the owner of sky-

Khashoggi ... seized

scraper blocks in Manhattan which Marcos had bought with looted money.

The racket was allegedly set up to hide the sacked dictator's massive assets.

Khashoggi also arranged to "sell" millions of pounds' worth of art treasures held by Marcos which supposedly vanished when Marcos and his wife Imelda fled in 1986, it is claimed.

America gave the pair immunity, but indicted them when they realised the scale of their massive swindling.

Most of the loot they *Continued on Page Nine*

ATISH-OW!

A pillow feather made salesman Mark Meehan, 28, sneeze so violently he was taken to hospital at Dudley, West Midlands, with a suspected broken neck.

GATES OF HELL

• Some fans picked pockets of victims

• Some fans urinated on the brave cops

• Some fans beat up PC giving kiss of life

Opened the gate ... Superintendent Marshall

DRUNKEN Liverpool fans viciously attacked rescue workers as they tried to revive victims of the Hillsborough soccer disaster, it was revealed last night.

Police officers, firemen and ambulance crew were punched, kicked and urinated upon by a hooligan element in the crowd.

Some thugs rifled the pockets of injured fans as they were stretched out unconscious on the pitch.

By HARRY ARNOLD and JOHN ASKILL

In one shameful incident, a gang of Liverpool fans noticed that the blouse of a girl trampled to death had ridden above her breasts.

As a policeman struggled in vain to revive her, they jeered: "Throw her up here and we will ... her."

Sheffield officers have been talking among themselves about the crush — and their boss Supt Marshall — who gave the order to open the gates because he was worried

STUNG

about the crush OUTSIDE the ground.

And yesterday, as the death of a 14-year-old boy brought the toll to 95, they too were back.

One fervent policeman, who witnessed Saturday's carnage stormed: "As we struggled to revive those in the front, Liverpool fans — just feet away — were jeering.

"As we struggled to revive them, appalling conditions became very tense, fans standing further up the terraces were openly urinating on us and on the bodies of the dead.

"And as policemen on the pitch tried to save lives, the yobs were jeering. *Continued on Page Two*

DI GRIEVES FOR LEE, AGED 14: Pages 2 and 3

With regards to what I write in this book, what parts of it are my real life views and what parts of it are just for entertainment?

The dialogue that criticises the Propaganda State/Propaganda Matrix are my views.

The Peoples Courts are not my view.

The Constitution guaranteeing relative equality (as outlined towards the end of the short story) is what I support. Discussion, differences of opinion, decision making should be carried out within that egalitarian and fair context.

I expect the UK (In terms of party politics) to follow the same path as Germany and France.

Printed in Great Britain
by Amazon

37600883R00059